# Verses of Another Kind

# RONALD BENJAMIN

Verses of Another Kind
Copyright © 2022 by Ronald Benjamin

All rights reserved. No part of this publication may be reproduced, distributed, or transmitted in any form or by any means, including photocopying, recording, or other electronic or mechanical methods, without the prior written permission of the author, except in the case of brief quotations embodied in critical reviews and certain other non-commercial uses permitted by copyright law.

Tellwell Talent
www.tellwell.ca

ISBN
978-0-2288-6916-0 (Hardcover)
978-0-2288-6915-3 (Paperback)
978-0-2288-6917-7 (eBook)

## Table of Contents

Author .............................................................................. 1
Woe on Earth ................................................................... 2
Chicken Scratching ........................................................... 4
Nobody at Heart ............................................................... 5
The Next Gen ................................................................... 7
Aviators ............................................................................ 9
Midhairies ....................................................................... 11
Financial Furore .............................................................. 13
My Resume ..................................................................... 15
Saga Down Under ........................................................... 17
The Wet .......................................................................... 20
Daylight Raving .............................................................. 21
Taboo Club ..................................................................... 22
Man Boobs ..................................................................... 24
What Ifs .......................................................................... 25
Playing Hooky ................................................................ 26
Rat's Arse Club ............................................................... 28
HooGow ......................................................................... 30
Walkabout ...................................................................... 31
Med Science ................................................................... 33
Nursing About ................................................................ 35
Fluffy Stuff ..................................................................... 37
Curly Cop ....................................................................... 38
Mother Boats .................................................................. 40
Rex Gets Lucky .............................................................. 41
Scrubs ............................................................................. 43

| | |
|---|---|
| Skunks Working | 44 |
| The Calathumpian | 46 |
| Lines of Thought | 47 |
| Welcome | 50 |
| Cactus Club | 51 |
| Cactus Club Membership | 54 |
| Solomon Lingo | 55 |
| High School Pranks | 56 |
| Playing Trains | 58 |
| Cooktown Times | 60 |
| Star Wars Correspondent | 63 |
| How to Lose Friends and Alienate People | 66 |
| Rural Life | 68 |
| Tributes | 70 |
| The Peaceful Pilot | 70 |
| "Flyer" | 71 |
| Happy Landing Joy | 72 |
| Mardi | 73 |
| The Port Moresby Gliding Club | 75 |

# Author

Ronald Benjamin Pearce; born and raised in Sydney. Early years attended technical college. Worked and contracted in the building industry before gaining a Commercial Pilots licence. Flew aerial survey aircraft for seven and a half years on operations all over Australia, New Guinea and the Solomon Islands before moving to North Queensland and starting my own air charter and air tour operation as well as a building business, the family by then had four boys. A life of diversity and adventure enjoyed with many stories latent therein.

Poetry; at times driven by life from day to day or events along the way. Then it must sometimes just be to have one's say. By inspiration brought on by a whim or just dreaming at night. Can be inspired with a thought that just comes out of nowhere without a care. Readers will have to follow suit to get the gist and enjoy the bliss.

It can be in Couplet, Narrative to some extent, in Rhythm at best by me, Sonnet could be. Then maybe not.

Cheers

# Woe on Earth

There came a time on earth when man's life
stood still all because a virus made us ill.

It travelled through the air out to sea and
everywhere. Stopped us flying the world around
with all the airlines stuck on the ground.

The cruise we took the world to look, went from a dream
to nightmare when so many aboard got crook.

Confined to cabin, home isolation or quarantine
most distressing but so it's been, fourteen days off
the scene. Unsociable distancing is so mean.

Could be at its worst if over the hill with many ending up
in boot hill, but for others there was reprieve with willing
help from medics and many others rolling up their sleeves.

No going to the pub to shoot the breeze with your mates, your
fevered sport or footy match, they've shut the bloody gate.

Fitness classes and treadmill at the gym no more,
they have cleared the floor. Those massage rubs
and bobble tub have now all been scrubbed.

Bathing at Bondi Beach with family, build a sand-
castle or surf a breaker is out of reach. Getting
spliced or planted with only a few allowed around
means you'll have to do it twice to get a crowd.

Shopping now is in a panic, stockpiling vitals, coughing
pills and sanitising vapour, but don't expect to buy
any toilet paper. All that folding stuff is a No-No.
If you need to pay it must be tap and go.

Though keeping distance and borders closed
had the world economy on the nose, with lots of
industry and businesses forced to close?

Out of work and on the bread line, for many the sun
no longer shines. Retirement fund and leave will take
a hit, but heaven help if you're without any of it.

At least it has come at last all governments are in the
one class, keen to support health recovery, the economy
and legislation measures pass. Approve new vaccinations
and give a jab to everyone across the nation.

But will the wheel go around and see us with our feet
back on the ground, standing high and wondering
for why? such woe in Earth and what in the world
happened to that other guy? Only heaven knows.

Then, after all, there could a little bliss… with time for more
than just a kiss, one might expect before too long baby will come
along Ho-Ho followed by a boom instead of all that gloom.

# Chicken Scratching

Literature is advancing in many strange and diverse ways since technology took precedence over teachings of olden days.

Writing has become more like scribble and spelling less than best when thumbing out that text.

For the younger generations…it can be done with lightning speed…slogans and all the rest, though for those with a grasp of old-style writing, it's looking like a mess, one can only guess?

Google may save the day, as long as they are here to stay, with global reach, knowledgeable verse, photos and video too it's all about the universe, but lookout for the sin, as for the dictionary and encyclopaedia go, might as well chuck them in the bin.

No need at all to be at one's desk, with tablets and mobile phone you can be in just about any zone. That is, long as you are not behind the wheel, driving in a car on the phone.

For talking is distractive from the traffic scene, texting is a danger that could send you off the road. "MUM! I just woke up in hospital, I must have had a crash? Don't know how long I've been there, but the doctors say from now on I'll need a wheel-chair."

Expressions are the go whether graffiti on the wall, by email, texting images and all that patching but for heaven's sake, why? Chicken Scratching.

# Nobody at Heart

In a World of fame and fortune of celebrities and esteem one is expected to realise that lifelong dream.

'Twas one such individual who did the ladder climb, making nothing into millions, while the sun never stopped to shine.

The spirit of adventure laid The World at his feet, while the sky was not the limit with The Universe on the beat.

And they did say he came from nothing just a no-body with no past how could his lavish lifestyle ever last?

From Las-Vogues or Paris, with the elite or Royalty to be seen. But they must pay him homage whether President or Queen.

The paparazzi must pursue with everlasting zest to get that elicit photo for a scoop in gossip press.

Private jetting here and there or sailing majestically on the Med so neat, caviar and champagne just to give the feast a bit of lust let it be a treat.

The ladies so pretty, neat and trim…though in a huff at the slightest whim. Cocktails in the pool just to toast their luck and my God… look at those bikinis…so weenie.

But "Oh" alas the pace is daunting, pressure's always on to keep the business rolling and make the show go on and what if Wall Street crumbles and comes crashing at one's feet, there'll be little in the pocket and nothing left to eat.

On the run to escape investors and face up for fraud much worse. Or jumping out a window, then riding in a hearse.

He could become homeless, just a has-been on the street, but maybe it would be better without all the stress and strain to just get back to basics and a simple happy life again, so sweet.

In the hope of peace and leisure how could he get off this tether, for his youthful days still haunt him… as when there was nothing to taunt him.

Old times when the loyalty of family and friends would never end. Mum and Dad whilst ever poor never wavered in their chores making sure there was always good food on the table and going in one's jaws.

No worries or obligations to stop him go fishing or for a swim with the girls and boys in the creek without a cossie or a care.

When just being Joe-Blow like everyone else the go whilst at the pub with the boys all broke, to have a beer and crack a joke and at the girls that pass on by a little whistle for a smile and a wink of the eye.

It's best of all to go with one's heart and what you always know, just back to basics, being a nobody the way to go.

# The Next Gen

Adam and Eve… if you believe first generation of God's creation, then again, one might think it was the missing link

Was man's beginning so sublime with Garden of Eden and life so fine, or did he first make the scene when getting out of the trees and standing up to see with ease

The Missing Link there must have been but they are nowhere to be seen. Neanderthals then trod the earth and helped pave the way for Homo Sapiens to spread far and wide

In any case, it wasn't long before new babies came along, the Next Gen ever keen to learn as much as quick can be, make home in cave, build one out of mud and bark or float off in The Ark, each New Gen has left its mark

On cave walls, stones and scrolls, building bridges, pyramid and Sphinx, writing with quill and ink, ever onwards through the ages learning more and more by civilisation and war, each new lot giving their best shot

Till at last they are defined; as Baby Boomers, Gen X, Y and Z, but not without a shove from Gen War making up for lost time with love, did Baby Boomers soar above all odds, growing up to captain industries and nations, would like to set kids up ahead but spending their inheritance instead.

Gen Y or Millenniums in their majority have the bit and the race is on, must keep up the pace with latest technology ever on, can't wait, must have biggest and best, not heed cost, take all the risk, into debt up to neck "what the heck"

Millenniums not so sure regard big business and politicians with suspicion not happy with war missions, fights for human rights and energy reforms, worry that the planet warms, like to see a world of change to kickoff next thousand years with a cheer

New arrivals on the planet Gen Z take first step into the world but is it all that real, overrun with a myriad of gadgets and little interest in playing with ball, then again gaming apps to fixate on and social media to make friends at a great rate

They can reach both near and far connecting even with their stars, though must be aware not to let aliens in intent on sin

After Z we now are back to Alpha, so then what comes next, will aliens from out of space take over the place or does it all start from the beginning again with God's creation and promise eternal life, As long as there's not apple bite or once again there'll be strife

Perhaps it could stay a planet of the apes, or could we at last see that missing link chased out or the threes by that "satin serpent" potting on the squeeze if you please

In any case it must be said they will need eyes in the back of their head

# Aviators

Aviation has been a passion since Pterosaurs took to the air, Birds and Mites took flight leaving man stock grounded in disappear seeing flying foxes up there

There was some latent progress when boomerangs took flight but no one knew the secret among other things as to how man could git up in the air… without growing wings

Aeons later balloons began to float, gliders sailed a little way but didn't stay; so many attempts came and went so hell bent no reward just yet

Powered flight was the answer propelling string and bag machines through the air… for any chance to stay at height and landing without a fright.

Adventure then began to see how far man could go in this new contraption and give the spectators a show

But little did they know before decades were over they'd be making record flights and fighting deadly air battle scenes in the latest air machines.

Then atomic times begin, flying Super Forts drop The Bomb, air fleets grow massive, Arms Race and Cold War on, the chopper makes its first dance, such marvels in advance

Space race full on, when the Russkies start putting on the pace, Sputnik first satellite to orbit Earth, then doggie Laika beating man into space… What a disgrace…..

Jet Age then a wonder with speed of sound and noise like thunder, air force, airline in their wondrous big aircraft are winging ever onwards, never thinking of the past

Aviation is a passion that pulls the heart strings for hang gliding, aerobatics, air racing and airline wings

Pilots are a breed alone that take to the sky as a home, though they are not alone, many others are in the wiz, it takes air crew, engineers, controllers and the lot to get a passenger to go up without a fear, asked "coffee, tea or milk?" "No thanks, I will have a beer."

Now that is not the end of pace with ever on the space race, stepping foot upon the Moon, before too long living on Mars, to outer space and the stars…

## Midhairies

*There is nothing as catastrophic*
*Or has raised the fear of millions*
*Than the horror of a mid-air collision*
*But you haven't felt the hackles*
*And your hairs stand on end*
*Till you've had the rude awakening*
*Of a near miss in mid-air*

*It can happen in an instant*
*With such shock and surprise, that*
*It will leave you cold and shaken*
*While the adrenalin multiplies*

*One must never take for granted*
*That the sky is yours alone*
*For there are possibly others*
*Boring holes that no-one knows*

*You can be alert and scanning*
*Where the traffic is expected*
*Yet find your starboard window*
*Full of onward rushing air machine*

*Though your action in an instant*
*Does in a split second save the day*
*The loud BRRROooff as it passes over*
*Makes you the whites and dismayed*

*Ronald Benjamin*

*Yet it may be in the outback, where*
*There is no highway in the sky*

*That you spot a Neptune bomber*

*Just half a mile away*

*Though is seems of little conflict*
*You had better be aware*
*For the rapid rate of closure*
*Quickly uses up the air*

*It will need best aerobatics*
*To avoid catastrophe*
*Then fly on shaken, thanking*
*Heavens you eyed the sky to see*

*You will never ever after*
*Feel alone when you go up there to fly*
*While your eyes can't stop flashing*
*Between the latest technical instruments and that*
*Panoramic windscreen less it's not just full of sky*

# Financial Furore

Now our financial institutions have for long been above all us rest and their shareholding amidst the very best, dividends and earnings sky high ever on

Whilst the top executives had a go at taking out the dough, big salaries in the millions, huge bonuses all the go and don't forget golden handshakes in case they might run low

Being CEO or on The Board no doubt is worth reward, but is it really justified when permitting scams and fraud to ride, adding to rewards?

For clients interest rates are first set to fit their wallet. Then the rate goes up and up with a wallop and a surprise to open both their eyes

If they're late that's just great, it opens the gate, with more profit on the make and that advice given so freely has set the Corporation up to make the chart hit the ceiling

The livestock so fat, the crops are high, small business booming the rewards high. Though home prices so dear loans are millions with no fears the owner takes a lifetime debt on and gives a big cheer

"Oh" alas home prices plunge, the sky stays blue for years on end, the stock they starve… the fields are dry… small business struggles…the bills roll in… penalty interest rates apply… some wish they could die……

Still you must pay or they take the place away, shut the door to your store, out on the street so to speak a lifestyle and all positions gone in a week

The credit cards are at their max, with interest rates that make heads spin so, all you think is chuck them in the bin…

Never mind whether flood or drought, financial crisis world throughout, finance freeze and on their knees, the Federation will bail the Board out if you please, so they can just lift their snout, while all them losing are left without

A Royal Commission might be the go, make those greedy "So and Sos" tell and show, just why they shouldn't be hung out to dry, for making piles and clients cry

Though would it help in the end, if the authority is but a friend, unlikely to take the sword and get stuck into rogue boards and have the institutions make amends?

# My Resume

Please accept this application for the position at the top, with my primest best intentions, "though I don't mind a drop."

I have travelled willy-nilly and experienced quite a lot, though at times lucky not to get shot

You can rest assured as chairman of the board, there will be perks all around and cover-up for fraud

My education; has been extensive, attending Two-Up and Reform School, furthered in aviation crashing on first solo flight, cattle duffing learnt to ride at night

Surgery was a delight till that tom pussy took-off in fright, sedation such a cinch when downing Martini those ladies loved a pinch

I defended well in law, leaping six-foot paling fence, with security in the bank quick on the draw, "hands up get on the floor??"

As a snoop there was no equal, Sherlock in a pram, I could sniff out a suspect wealthy client, on a Paris roundabout in a jam

Rocket Science was a blast, sending cane toads to the moon, so fast!

Professionally; I have excelled at plundering in the Caribbean, getting ladies like Cleopatra into bed while floating on the Med and in Vegas you can bet it will be sweet, because cheating is a treat

Sports; fight like hell, on the ropes till ring the bell. Down back allies retreat full speed, a mugging didn't need

Particulars are; age all in the past just hope it will last, birth at home in the bush with mum's big push, mirage what a fast never last, wives think no more than two? At a time! Family what a chore and in the way, alimony no pay

Other interests and activities; are high on the agenda, like strip clubs, cruising bars, sunbaking on Waikiki or at Moulin Rouge in Gay Paree, at Monaco water ski

To Whom it Will Concern                Faithfully Yours: Sexy Rex

Reference attached:

Have long known Rex, and see he is capable of anything! I have long followed in his footsteps, unfortunately always one step behind

I have no hesitation in recommending this "So and So" for the gallows, he is the source of much strife and has now run off with my wife! Better Luck,

Mad Hopping

# Saga Down Under

Since days when Cook onboard Endeavour set sight on these shores, there have been changes by the scores

With London full of felons and nowhere else to go… the judiciary had their say, "ten years hard labour transportation, Botany Bay"

Then Captain Phillip on arrival took one look and said, "No-good we will go to Port Jackson and settle Sydney Cove instead!"

Soon growing with new convict arrivals coming ashore, under whips and harsh laws, roughing it up at The Rocks with the Rum Corps

Exploring the big challenge taken as intrepid as can be, to lands South then West and coast by sea, Settlers in their haste clearing out farmland, pioneers on expeditions venture far and wide across outback lands

Towns and land holding growing ever more, under pressure ever on to find workforce, funds to carry on, build roads for Cobb & Co, Bullock Teams and so, for the pace is always on

"Eureka" the cry when eyesight big nugget met, the news soon gets around, hopeful prospectors arriving in a rush from worldwide old towns, big nuggets to be found.

From Europe, America, Asia and jumping ship, out to gold fields eagerly they spread wide along bush track with gold pan, shovel and haversack on their back

Governor in a flap looking to get his bit makes law, for you to dig in gold pit must have ten pound permit. "Too much" the diggers cry, protests and set permits afire

Authorities not impressed intent on rebel leaders arrest; in defiance Diggers build stockade, standing firm on their ground will not pay that ten pound

Troopers then sent in with bayonets fixed against stockade, Diggers guns and picks; before next morn legend is born

Rascals become legend too with bushranging all the go, Kelly boys, Ben Hall gang and Captain Moonlight being just a few, with daring bank raids and stage holdups their domain, they shout "Stick'em Up" before escaping to the hills with the gold and all the bills.

Nation building well in hand Federation granted without a fight. Roads and railway spread throughout the land Cities grow at an expeditious rate, life is great…

Empire then again at war with volunteers in demand, call on the colonies to fill the ranks, so many Diggers join the kill and go, Gallipoli, France and so the legend grows

Outback holdings in hundreds of square miles. Graziers are all smiles; nation riding on sheep's back, overlanders droving big cattle herd down along paddock cattle track, QANTAS founders get off the ground, flying doctor makes the rounds

Not always was it so good, with worldwide depression at the door, no work no pay, must work for dole or hit the road, hump the bluey, get hand out for chopping wood or jump the rattle freight trains, go interstate cut cane for low pay rate

Once again The Empire is in the tin, help is needed or the enemy will win, off once more to fill the ranks, hold Tobruk, fly with Air Force, sail Navy ships, nursing wounded and much more World War. Stopping Tojo at the door, Spitfires over Darwin, Battle Coral Sea, Kakadu Track and Timor Sparrow Force not without remorse

Immigration then a must to give a growing nation thrust. Skilled workers in demand, European immigrants, war refugees welcome in, ten-pound Poms all ship over, there is work on Snowy Scheme and country all over

Of course there is much more in the past and in store, "so bring it on," advance the nation fair some more, uphold the legends one and all recall the swaggie down bay the billabong and sing "Waltzing Matilda" song.

# The Wet

Wet season is a blessing for thirsty north tropic lands,
it flushes out the rivers and soaks wide spans of land,
freshens up rainforest makes waterfalls everywhere

A welcome relief from the overbearing dry heat that can
be so oppressive it can knock one off your feet

The younger generation take delight while splashing at play while primary
producers brace the bar with shouts all-round and give a big hurrah

But "Woe" there could be cyclones that trash in from the sea…
devastating crops… destroying towns and city, flooding may
be horrendous inundating farms, homes and shops owners
left with little, cleaning up with trucks and mops

Transport can be stranded, trucks and trains stopped
everywhere and motorists' best not drive into flooding
waters for fear of sinking car and drowning there

Cyclone reconstruction flood clean-up costly taking sometimes
years, land and rainforest live on again through another year

Living in the tropics is an awesome way of life, one must expect
though a bit of strife, it comes and goes as everyone knows

A helping hand will be on call from your neighbour big or
small and when all done it's back to fun, out on the reef,
up on dancing feet for in the tropics life is sweet

# Daylight Raving

To wake up in the morning without the urge to yawn
before the birds are chirping must be a nature warn

Our tourist in their way must wonder in dismay why
that promised daily lark must start off in the dark

In East on sea the sun still to shimmer the reef
to see still dimmer, the West in dark they do
wonder if the Lord has made a blunder

The penguins in their suits down South think
it's great, they don't wake up till late

Our work must be done on time so first takeoff with a burst,
leave Mum and family in a muddle and so much for that cuddle

As day wears on those busy carry on till that universal moment
sun still sky high the day is then done, but don't worry
you now can have some rest, or must we have some fun

The penguins think it's great they can stay up till late

Sunlight does not a changing; us folks living nature's way, wish
the artificial flow would just get up early and give us all a go

# Taboo Club

*Thinking time to put roots down, Rex perused sleazy parts of town, till at last the darkest den underground he found*

*This place might look the pits but all Paris will be in despair after I fix it up a bit, fill it with tits and call it Taboo without a care*

*It will be exclusive in its clientele and before they know it they'll be under my spell, will need a pass to get in, bulging wallets and sly grin. Bouncers looking like totems will frisk you at the door and boot you out if make uproar*

*In Taboo you will be chaperoned close along by our escorts all night college taught, first drink will be on the house, formulated above all rest, down the hatch "Cocktail Rex" best*

*After that the bar will be yours with a tab, tick it all up, no need to know the price will tell them when the cards all gone, eats will be served with a smile just might have to wait a while, to be as ordered served in dim light, 'it's yours! Just take a bite'*

*For all those who would like to make a bet there will be a shady room out the back where they can have a crack, on the tote Rex will take a wager but might not be there when time to pay ya*

*You can deal a deck of cards, turn up a top hand, eager to play but better be aware we will have mirrors here and there using drink try, roulette and bandits will be in Rex's favour, then they will think I'm getting free drink, If just by chance they do win big we'll drive them home like a rocket on the way picking pocket*

*Floor show goes on set to stun, all the girls on stage clobber they will have next to none long legs kicking high, Zara fabulous as our star Delilah on a par with see-through veil and big red lips, sparkling glass ruby in her middle, tassels on other bits and you can't believe those snake-like swivel hips*

*Stud Power act starring Sexy Rex, Bad Bar Boys all the rest, intended for making ladies in a trance, drinking up, scream for more, dance till all hang out for more and knickers on the floor*

*Guest can get up on stage; have a go all the rage, under hypnotic trance made to dance, like a duck "quack – quack" with open eye, voodoo doll first prize*

*So the show will go on all night not a clock in sight, till at last we sweep them out the door, full as a boot into bright sunlight, poor as a church mouse will probably have to sell the house.*

## Man Boobs

*Man boobs are a bonus*
*That are due to good life and happy wife*
*They come in your autumn*
*Not like young ladies*
*That blossom in the Spring*
*They along with other bulges*
*Brought on by grub and beer*

*Not like baby bumps*
*Those are due to sex with no fear*
*For it will be gone within a year*

*With futility over time*
*They show off one's stance*
*Though maybe not one's social advance*

*But where would you be without them*
*As skinny as a rake, for heaven's sake?!*

# What Ifs

*If the world had been flat, Columbus would have been first man in space.*

*Without invention of the wheel there would be no
need for speed, cars, trains or planes.*

*Living forever man's great wish granted, if Eve had not eaten
that apple, next not to age a blow, no show, when departed
pray for Heaven's bliss, or will it be the devil's kiss.*

*If we had never fought a war what other chaos would be in store?*

*Yes! If Pigs can fly – 'you tell a lie.' Pigs arse – 'what a laugh.' Bringing in the
bacon – 'giving pay-check to the wife'. Ham in pea soup – 'I am lost in thick
fog.' Ham sandwich – 'a punch in the mouth.' Roast pork – 'hawk the fork.'*

*If the world suddenly stood still, would we all fly off
into space or have to race to keep up the pace?*

*If you must take the plunge to save poor he or she,
first ask yourself, "What's in it for me?"*

*If not take care of yourself, don't expect that all others will be there.*

*If one goes to war to even the score, on home front shut the door.*

*if Cupid didn't have an arrow we would be on the straight
and narrow, Romeo would give Juliet a miss, unless Venus and
Aphrodite were to bless, making us eager to undress*

# Playing Hooky

Strolling happily on his way Prof passed two young lads going other way, one turned around just to say "Wagging it is Fun" intending to see Prof's shock and dismay.

In an instant it all came back to mind… the memory of those times "Yes, I remember" the reply, with look of surprise and open eyes the lad passed the news on to his mate, then they were gone.

Prof wondered, are they really having fun, or just getting out of school without a plan, not like we did so long ago in our troop. Prof, Baz, Chook, Tody and Man.

Rowboat fishing on River George, competition for biggest one, maths add up jelly fish, raid Luigi's watermelon farm along the way meaning no harm.

Luigi chasing off fire shotgun in the air, run like wild goat back to boat, second blast from the gun, Baz trips gives a yell crashes to the ground and then plays dead, troops gather round adding to the lark, Luigi collapse with shock… Baz he has shot, sees it's all put on, jumps up in a rage and troops charge off in retreat, next page.

No attending to have more sport or lean boring studies so thought, stay on school train and take a hike into Town Hall to explore the City, further education best intent, see art galleries masterpieces on show, museum exhibits of all kind taken in to pass the time the go.

Asked "Who you with?" not a problem, joining in with school group from out of town, "We're with them" would get a pass to listen in on lectures about displays, their-archaeology-skeletons and see stuffed animals' look of dismay!

Geography a favourite subject too. See Chinatown, Hyde Park, Kings Cross, The Bridge and Luna Park for a lark without forking out a penny. A trip to the Zoo, see the jumbos, lions and what those monkeys can do.

Newsreel Theatres give good lesson on latest affairs, villains and polar bears. Spend an hour cost half price when made to pay or slip in for free when usher away.

Of course there was time for shopping and have a test, David Jones have the best lot, try on jeans and corduroy jackets and go quick before floor manager makes a racket.

Honing skills in Central Fun Parlour arcade, use half penny in slot machine filed down to shilling size to win free game prize all well and good.

Unless truant officer Ted checks it out on a raid, in which case you better bolt, no missing out on sport, from parlour streak log George Street all way to Circular Quay with that Ted fleet of foot on your tail looking to nail you come what may.

Till at last there is a chance to stay at bay, Manly Ferry is about to on its way, all aboard just in time but so is Ted at last minute, not all lost, "Abandon Ship" troops leap back on dock. Ted off to Manly instead right on time with ship's clock. Spitting chips all the way vowing to nab those rascals next day.

End of day jump train, ride track back home on time, must now cover own tracks, get girlfriend to write neat note will do the trick, "He was away being sick"

Playing Hooky now put to bed, taking sicky day off instead

# Rat's Arse Club

Many moons ago when aeroplanes where still pretty new there was one enterprise set to show the way starting operations from a field near Botany Bay

A flying school was the go first up, then it all was set to grow with air services they were set to glow, airways in the sky would be next forte, selling seats from Sydney down to Bega adding to their pay

With being in the air they needed a name with some flare to take them fare no matter how hard. "Adastra" it will be! "Through Adversity to the Stars" would fit well as time went past

Then came mapping from the sky, flying low, flying high, looking for minerals in pay dirt or photo mapping Mother Earth ranging far and wide did they search, operating many different aircraft, flown by a bevy of crew all united as one and didn't mind a bit of fun

In the field it was full-on when sun came up to beat the cloud and air bumps, then back to base, could be some-way out place, then a nap and a bite before some fun at night, dance and sing, have a beer, give the boss a cheer

Not all would go so well with crashes there is hell, leaving all somewhat aghast wishing they could change the past

But what the hell they must go on back in the air on another run, those that have had their day would see it all that way; though forget them not old friends of many a day for one could be with them any day.

We Adasrians will gather round to cheer our old mates at the pub and in remembrances of them will call the group Rat's Arse Club and go on flying in no fear and not give a rat's arse as long as our days and years are here.

For the fortunes of joining Adastra Air and Ground Crew you could gain the privilege of being member of Rat's Arse Club too

Rules as they may be say you must have been an expatriate, expired or now doing as Adasrians do. Exceptions there are few

And so as time moves on when others are gone to get their wings at the Pearly Gates, a Keg of Honour is put on. Amen

## HooGow

Looking up at the cloud some wonders
How much their shape abounds
What within can be found

You might see shapes so weird
That looks like faces in the sky
Creatures that could be from a zoo
Sharks, dragons, elephants on the fly too

Then you could look within
Riding on a beast made from tin
But be aware there are strong forces
That will scare, monsters do abound

Can be in form of lightning flash, ice and
Turbulence severe, no need to despair
A good one is there that will take care

"HooGow" mythical monster
Hiding in the clouds
Is there to see you safe at play

Making cloud shapes every which way
You must look for HooGow
In the clouds every day

# Walkabout

Once upon dreamtime lots of centuries ago, there
was a land about who nobody knows, except for
tribes of native nomads living their traditional way,
bushcraft skills practised for ever and a day

They could live on yams, witchetty grub, goannas,
bush tucker and kangaroo, needing very little
clobber to see the day, night through

Gunyah shelter made from bark, just in case they
blow away, for they could build a new one very next
day, or just move into a cave with nothing to pay

Spears tipped with sharp stone gave the hunt good range
while creeping up in disguise… to better the surprise…

Long ranging no problem flock attack sent skyward with
boomerang coming back if the birdies didn't get a whack

History being recorded forever and a day by painting rock
art and having it on display like hunting trophies so to say

Corroborees to uphold their manly stance, body well-painted
for the occasion and to initiating of the boys, rainbow serpent,
bunyips and that legend to be taught, didgeridoo and clicking
sticks setting pace for the gig, stamping feet to the beat

Ladies are forbidden to attend… having secret
business of their own of all sorts, lap-lap only needed
for best dressed, baby in bilum on the chest

Cultural understanding of the kind set so tribal life
kept fine, must knowing firsthand less pointing bone
make one sick, or it could be your end if kadaicha
man was on the loose in his feather boots

Fishing from a bark canoe or hollow log so nice,
barramundi on the spear lots of geese in the air only
the crocodile to fear, Days, weeks, years go by there
is no difference in time as long as they beware

Keeping warm at night by the fire started by rubbing
sticks, with flickering light the place lit up keeping
snakes at bay while dingo pups can stay

Calling up rellies easy as pie with Bull Roarer wheeling in the
sky, smoke signal beacon the way to home them in, no need
for mobile phone if too far away send message stick anyway

Mode of transport on the hoof throughout the bush and
for vacation you may ask where that fellow went?

You know! He gone walkabout long time ago.

# Med Science

Starting out as witchcraft and as the domain of medicine men, med science is like magic that keeps one well and thin

Can be by spell or potion, placebo and willpower, in the form of penicillin or ground up Frog Powder… to make you feel better one way or other. Then on the other hand make you groan with tummy pain and dashing to the throne

Scientific studies of old risky business, against religious will, repercussions could be tragic, must use oneself as guinea pig, surgery most intrepid only for the brave, ever more so at night when digging up a grave, cadaver in short supply for fear scalpel work post-mortem still might hurt

In war and peace, sick and wounded suffer plague and neglect until Pasteur, Curie, their like and Nightingale's work take effect. The scene is set to raise the bar in labs and hospital wards near and far. X-ray and scan they see within.

Surgery advance a marvel with organ transplant, dialysis, scans, radiation therapy of all sorts, no longer wooden leg prosthetic one instead. Ology Specialists of all sorts have their sway

Nursing has as always been full on, taking care of your needs till you're gone. If you need one just press the bell if wet the bed what the hell, they will give your blood pressure a check and now like all else nursing has gone Hi-Tec

Pharmaceuticals expand at will, creating potions to help live longer, ever more pills to take and jabs for Heaven's sake, but are they all that safe?

Love life can be enhanced though with a good shot. Ladies on the pill no baby bump no care, men on big dose of Viagra giving lots of joy. Might go tits up out with a bang "Oh Boy!"

# Nursing About

*Like Aunty Mavis a nurse young Mac just had to be*
*To help the ill and World to see*
*With that all in mind she did the ladder climb*
*By learning well and working hard*
*For her studies the reward was great*
*Helping mothers have babies that just can't wait*
*Maturity being her specialty, way outback or overseas*
*Though like Auntie's travel bug she got the bite.*
*So off backpacking it was to Europe to see the sights*
*In New Guinea spruiking pidgin she applied her skills*
*As midwife, on bush clinics giving jabs and Quinine pills*
*First Port Moresby, then Goroka and Lae on the job*
*Then it was Bob that made Denise's heart throb and say "I Do"*
*She would willingly take on new tasks*
*Even help building their own Ark*
*Then as time passed on back to "OS" all family on board*
*Intrepid as can be they set off to sail the Coral Sea*
*Back on dry land in Cairns they decided to make a stand*
*With lots of jobs and high schools at hand*
*But nursing is what Denise really liked to do*
*Cairns Base took one look and said we'll have you*
*And so it was for many long days and years*
*Taking on many a new challenge in maternity and childcare*
*That travel bug then seemed to grow with each bite*
*So off to Africa on safari to see lions, elephants and all the sights*
*Back on deck at Cairns Base there was pickup in pace*

*With a need to answer the demand for child cancer care*
*In administration and to be at hand, here there and everywhere*
*Till at long last regretfully like all one becomes a retiree.*
*A book to Write for the World to see*

## Fluffy Stuff

Each day as Sadie sweeps and cleans

Till not a speck of fluff to be seen

Then there is a basket full that needs Wash and dry

Into the tub for a scrub, no way

Washing machine will save the day

In no time flat it's out, but what is that?

Fluffy Stuff is everywhere about

No matter how hard she tries

Those tissues do their trick

Spread through the wash wide and thick

Washed as clean as can be

But awful hard to get free

Shake and flap as much can she

Sadie sure she checked the pockets??

No point getting in a rage

Look at all that clean spare change

# Curly Cop

*Curly Cop is all about, at The Station is full on*
*Likes a joke about what's on and ply the clown*

*On the beat keeping watch just*
*To see where those crooks might be*
*If not good then on the spot*
*Off the watch house, in the dock*
*The magistrate to see and pay penalty*

*His special skill is on motorbike*
*Traffic patrol a delight*
*Here and there giving "P" platers a stern grin*

*Break the rules, use phone, run the Red*
*Stop for Curly's flashing lights instead*
*"You were speeding!"*
*"No, just going fast to get past."*
*"Now you will be last!"*
*Ticket on the spot, lost points and empty purse*
*Passengers not impressed and think you silly*
*Not best. Fail driving test*

*Up and down the Highway Bruce the go*
*Out to Buskins Point for a look*
*Will nab those on the loose.*
*Where is that goose?*

*Verses of Another Kind*

*Speeding a big no-no consequence might be mortal blow*
*Must stop For Curly traffic cop*
*But "Oh" no off they go at frightening pace, it's a race*

*Down the road just like a rocket*
*Why do they try to get away?*
*Is it drink, car theft, popping pills or puffing weed*
*That makes them drive with no danger heed*

*Calls for backup and a chopper if you can*
*Road spikes and the lot*
*Or there might need to be a shot*
*To stop the "tommyrot"*

*Just another day Curly to all will say*
*Back at the station to report*
*Off home then to have a beer and the day*
*No more thought*

# Mother Boats

Marlin session challenge hard to describe, attracting game fisher from far and wide, keen to catch the biggest one, get photos, win trophy and first prize

Outside the reef they search up and down for days till all beat and a bit dizzy need some rest and something fizzy

Lucky Mother Boat is close at hand to save long trip back to dry land, with lots of room to party on, celebrate and kiss the girls. Coral Sea-tel, Mantaray, Majestic and such named, fun to board and without shame. Clebs like Marvin and his mates think it's all just great

Other fishers hard at work, catching crays, netting prawns way out to sea toiling under sunny sky or riding stormy seas, till bins are full and must unload, fill up with fuel, food and beer

While stuck at anchor to be on hand big supply barge with bearded crew reading Playboy and old books, biding time there weighting, feeling blue

Mother ship rendezvous bring the news, fresh food, fuel and some booze. Trawlers taking all their needs, unloading catch exchanging books and some crew

There will always be Mother Boats at sea; lugger tending pearl divers in their suits or as big pontoon out on the reef there for day trippers and scuba divers that don't need lead boots

# Rex Gets Lucky

Floating in the air a slip of paper drifted here and there… until at last it hit Rex in the face sleeping in the park and fell into his hand

He screwed it up in haste thinking it just waste, wasn't thinking of a bin, then sat up opened one eye, unfolded to read within, old lotto ticket some sod tossed away thinking it didn't pay, not intending stuck it in his pocket anyway

Then at the pub on the news there was wonder just who had that winning ticket from Down Under, with time to spare and clock stopped Rex checked the numbers and got a shock, ticking one at a time till they were all in a line, straight away needed a bottle of wine

In the morning I will see if all that moolah can be snatched by me. I will make a list of worthy causes, on what to spend and who to bring along, first crossing charity off the top, family - forget that lot - old friends if any, not a penny

There will be time to spree whilst cursing out to sea, in defiance of the rest of the world over the stern I will pee. Then I could buy a ticket for a trip around the moon, to see the other side, but not too soon

Instead it could be fun buy my own Superyacht and sail around the world, visit exotic places where few have ever been, dock in far out ports taking in the scene. I will have to have the best on board no holds barred I can afford

Crew will be recruited must have a shady past, captain will have to have skulduggery well in hand, mate adept at locating where plunder at, deckhands slick when on the nick and getting booty on board quick

Cabin crew will be the best on parade or undressed, selected always on merit and neatness, of ferret, then maybe I'll have a sugar baby, will need to be erotic to best please me, have big brown eyes or blue ones wide they are on the crew

Or give all that a miss, be a lone shark up to mean tricks, even start my own bank with a fortune to be made but wait I could lose the lot in a bank raid, be back in the park needing a shave

Better to plonk it all into my retirement investments funding that will attract oldies happy to put life savings in, from where without a qualm I can ever skim

At Lotto office first thing Rex rushed in to make a claim and hand ticket in, alas there was one hurdle yet to jump, proof of purchase… there needs to be… must explain where that be

Try his hardest Rex just could not say… no matter how hard he waved that; "winning ticket will win I say," till suddenly with a gust it blew away

# Scrubs

*That Scrubs is sneaky as can be snaking along
the trestles and up a palm tree*

*"Y" is looking long to see if she can catch that slippery
sod before disaster could be done My God…*

*Just where Oh where can that Python be? I'll get it good just
wait and see and into a sack that Scrubs will then be.*

*Then Jo Ho Ho off to Hartley's Zoo we will Go*

*Ssss Ssss*

# Skunks Working

I'll play to have some sucker away
Then down to the nitty gritty, when
I be one's self so shitty

We'll have them set us up as we ply
Then do our bloody best
To send them tits up and away

Just pass the poison round and
Heap the bullshit on too
Take the local in and hope
Hope those sucked in be gone

There'll be lots of help from mates
For sneakers they will be, by way in hand
I have the mugs believe in me
Loyalty and ethics to me don't matter

Alas the game not flash
The ship goes on we have not foreseen
The saps we thought would have been
Are still well on the scene

It seems this interlude we through
Just a little rude indeed, is not
Unusual to those with time in the business been

*It doesn't really matter*
*I'll just keep up the patter*
*And one day just slip away*
*The locals by then will say*
*How did he get to know*
*When he started out so low?*
*Skunk working it has been*
*For them to make the scene*

# The Calathumpian

*One's persuasion whether to politics or to a god*
*can be tricky and at times get quite sticky*

*Though the message from those at top and above*
*is all for the good and will fill the bill History has*
*not taught us don't war and each other kill*

*Some sects within each faction will not accept distraction*
*for fear of wronging and disparage others whilst singing*

*Whilst most will good doing, there are others not so fair of whom to*
*be aware being so wicked or maybe that destructive staunch bigot*

*As it all may seem a muddled-up bad dream, many*
*choose not to abide and keep an open mind being*
*Calathumpian as they may, liberal thinking their way*

*A philosophy of one's own, judgmental maybe not,*
*no faction to obey, seeing light at end of tunnel as*
*a win, if not in sight just chuck a big grin*

# Lines of Thought

*You will never know if you don't give it a go.*

*The higher you fly the further the fall.*

*When on the bones of your arse better the greener the grass.*

*When you dance love will advance*

*Living is dangerous, be aware take care.*

*Speed can give adrenalin or brain a burst, next feet first.*

*Loyalty best described as being one of the tribe.*

*Money you have you haven't, money you had you have.*

*Being wise will open eyes*

*Without gravity Universe would burst, nothing left on Earth.*

*Spend a penny in advance or might need clean underpants.*

*Didn't pay, bailiff on the way, beak will have sway.*

*Too much tension end up in mental attention*

*We all come to be and be gone the same way*

*Ronald Benjamin*

*E-technology poses big concern when
knowing the web is full of worms*

*It could have been worse, if run over by a hearse*

*Take a wife in for life*

*Reject marriage using undercarriage*

*Some laws can be an arse that blockheads pass*

*If you sin must kick in to the tin*

*Have a home with spouse but kids will get the house*

*Work just fills time in between bubble and strife*

*Blunders happen every day, say – Bugger…
Barambah… Cucumber…*

*Dating Sites say they get it right, when you
could get a big dinner night fright*

*When you don't like to get a yes or no, give ask a pass*

*Puppies with nice brown eyes a big surprise
when growing to man size*

*The dinner date will be a thrill till you have to pay the bill*

*Voted in with a promos and a grin, in
defeat kicked out for one's sins*

*A little bird flying by dropped a message in my
eye, thank heavens elephants don't fly*

*Getting older, time to think about the birds and the
bees flying by, and pray to heaven for your wings*

*As a prince once said! Two things most affecting us
today. The World fitness and mental climate*

*Whoever said, I never told a lie in my life will look
anyone straight in the eye, all except the wife*

*The devil looks after his-own, whether on the
take or the throne. God helps those that get caught
out, on their knees when saying please*

*Don't wake up when you dream, might interrupt
that pleasant scene or sit up with a scream*

*Things that go bump in the night. Not to worry.
Just hold onto partner good and tight*

*Preventing things that happened in the
past is in a short time just a farce*

*Worse things have happened but we don't know when*

*It's no-good apologising after you've spat the
dummy, the damage has already been done*

*The best doesn't always happen, but you must
make the best of what does happen*

*There is always a better way, even if it's the old way*

# Welcome

***Pleased to have you join in my birthday celebrations***
Eighty Years have come and gone
Since they had that little Ron

And in all that time a World to see
Over land in the air and out to sea

"Oh" what a time it has been
With lots of love and friendly teams
Though at times the ups and downs
Have left him with a frown
The wheel has always gone round
In a little while a smile

So here we are to give a cheer
Raise a glass and have a beer

Eighty Years have come and gone
But who knows for how long
So do the best one must
To make sure we don't rust

Let's mix it up and have some fun
But keep a foot on the next rung

**Buffet lunch and drinks on me**

# Cactus Club

Longing for adventure then there was no better place to make the scene, than when flying from Honiara's airstrip named "Cactus" by US Marines

Their adventure was exciting as possibly could be, make you green with envy and wish you had there been

Alas, for two decades the grass grows long till the UN came along taking once more to the air, to map for minerals, sending new air crew along. From Sweden six, all the way, Aussies two, US one and UK one to work and play

Flying most exciting, low over tropical isles up and down their rugged mountain range, just like riding on the tiger's tail could easily make one pale, after they would play and have a nip or to. Wasn't long before they were Cactus too

One was a lot put-off when his love was spurned, jumping into a plane and took-off, not being a pilot didn't matter he wasn't intending to land, just dive straight into the middle of town, end all when hit ground

To no surprise there was great concern, all knew kamikazes crash and burn, talk him down did take some persuasion, then sent off back to Sweden air express lucky not to be in straitjacket being Cactus new

Sent up north to get job done, alas there was no sun… down came tropical rain in tubs, stuck on ground for weeks on end, till news came there's going to be a dance. Queen's Birthday Ball big event of the year, only one chief pilot allowed to be sent

In Swedish there was one's outcry, no need to translate, "stick job in arse" Aussies say we're on strike if can't go pull the pin, project manager must give in, without a crew the whole operation is in the tin, so it came a chance to get to the big dance

At the G Club they walked in with a grin all set to commit sin, perfume in the air long dresses everywhere made their heads spin, free shouts at the bar by all that like to know "how's the flying all going," "are you going to crash?" "Going well," "We're not going to crash," stated with a sneer

Two bands banging out a turn Solomon Darkies and Deadbeats had all up for a trot, mixing it up lots, Happy Birthday Elizabeth the cheer most of her subjects half shot with not a care

Above all, her airmen on fire, intent on much damage and getting shot, crash and burn on the spot. Next day wake up all eyes red some can't get out of bed, grinning glances all round town. Back in the blue, no Cactus Club blues instead

Then one day not far away one has an invite to escort young lady fresh from college on night out, all goes well till on way home in the dark, stars glistening light the spark, young lady not just dizzy, at front door mum says "you're late" in a tizzy

Next day it hits the fan, in disgrace all over town, lass shipped out to religious house. Boss with a frown "what have you done?" "Nothing just had a kiss," might get the shove, no instead full membership Cactus Club…

Meanwhile back in Honiara plotting office scene one young Swede fell in love a lot and was set to tie the knot, though his Viking tradition upholding not to be forgot, kidnapped eve before wedding blindfolded for the flight made to scull strong liquid all that night

His whereabouts a mystery until suspects found, "do they ask for ransom before bringing him back to marry me?" the bride to be cried, no we'll have him there on time and own up to our crime, he'll need lots of coffee and a cold tub. Now office staff involved and all flyers, life members Cactus Club

Without a doubt the envy of all those except some vexed, not knowing what club had in plan next, lots of others nevertheless keen to lend a hand, meetings at the G Club could go on all night, flying as high as a kite, dance on table collapse it might

Till at last job is done and time to go, big send-off given to say goodbye. Room full of dignitaries and honoured guests all well-dressed. Some set to leave past one getting fresh air at the door when young lass hesitated to pass "suppose this is really goodbye."

"Aren't you going to give me a kiss?" he replied, in an instant she leaped like cougar to embrace, kiss sending them into outer space and over the moon only to land back on earth as naked as can be for all to see, a shove from mum out the door dad august mouth wide open as he passed. Cactus Club members for-ever more

**See novel**: *Three Kisses in Honiara*
Full story of this adventure.

# Cactus Club Membership

Open to all those with a worthy experience in naughtiness and notability as witnessed by their peers, and the good Lord.

Rules: One: - Whether on impulse or planned the qualifying event must be naughty enough to put your peers in a spin.

Two: - Be of no physical harm or suffer legal repercussions.

Three: - Good enough in retrospect to pardon and be upheld as a noteworthy act involving the participants.

Cactus Club Registration Application:-

E: members@cactusclubs.com

Nickname……………………………… Alias………………………

Hiding Place…………………………………………………………………

Contact, When Not About……………………………………………

Experience no holds barred……………………………………………

……………………………………………………………………………………

……………………………………………………………………Attach

Reproduction approvals regardless of time outrage or despair so incurred

x……………………………………… Life Membership: The X X Xs

## Solomon Lingo

What language of the Solomons?

Well it has only just begun.

For there are many different dialects

And a lot of foreign tongue

One Island on its own has some fifty different dialects and that is but a few

There is English - Pidgin – Chinese - Fijian and Japanese, all have added their bit as well

And if that is not enough

Then they're speaking Swedish too.

# High School Pranks

*In class there was an old white glass jar*

*Kept turning up despite teacher's orders "In the Bin"*

*Ernest being class bully on the large size*

*One that held his ground always keen to push around*

*Under desk old Vegemite jar he found*

*Good chance to put on a show*

*Opened jar and said "Oh Poo"*

*"Put that in the bin" teacher orders with a frown*

*"Yes Sir," out to impress whole class*

*On the way Ernest does ply and mess around*

*Holding nose, this and that way sway*

*"Sit down" teacher directs intent ending the act*

*"Yes Sir" returns to seat in same way*

*Chook; Sitting seat behind*

*About to implement stage two of plan*

*Places drawing pin squarely on Ernest's seat*

*Prof; Sitting across the aisle trying hard not to smile*

*With a sway Ernest turns and thumps down*

*Looking to pretend relief*

*Instead lets out an almighty yell, the world to tell*

*On his feet Oh so fast with both hands on his arse*

*Whole class has a laugh, got him back at last*

*Best ever act thanks to Vegemite and that little tack*

*Sir sends Ernest to get it mend*

*Then there must be revenge!*

*But just who is to blame?*

*Was it Chook that shook his head?*

*Or Prof, I have a grudge on instead*

*Ernest vows to make Prof pay*

*I'll break his neck and leave him a wreck*

*If I catch him in a corner his mother will be a mourner*

*Prof, not so easy to be caught, taunts Ernest as "Fat Slob"*

*For two weeks the chase is on all around sports ground*

*With Prof's evasive skills at the fore they went*

*Until at last as time went Ernest's energy is all spent*

# Playing Trains

From Regents Park the main line went south and
branch line through Bankstown to city going back.
As well there is a loop line going through to Chullora
marshalling yards so freight trains can pass too.

And in plum centre a big signal station to keep all
trains on right track, switching points and signals to
stop and go. For day and night the trains roll through,
a site for young kids that like a close up view.

From under low bridge between the tracks they could
take a peek with heads up through the sleeper to see trains
under gear and let out a scream that no one could hear.

Over branch line Chullora track Sydney water supply
pipeline goes, just the perfect place to have a lark. The
challenge is always on, who can make it to the top
of a water channel running down cutting side?

Four lads set they will give it another go at getting to the top,
across the track they will race. "Ready Set ------?" And three
take off full speed leaving Prof…standing in centre track…

Instinct made him look round and a big black freight
train his eyes found, no more than thirty yards away, fast
bearing down, driver and fireman hanging out each side

At rocket speed Prof's legs took off and took him right to
channel top… only one to get there with big freight train
thundering by behind, with whistle blowing all he could hear.

Just before time High School train due through Rego
station Melbourne Express streamline Thirty-Eight Zero
One comes flying through. All stand back as station master
says to stop from getting sucked in or blown away.

Though not Prof and Tody, they need a closer look and down
station end ramp they go. Can't there stand and be seen so on
bellies right next to tracks they are so keen to see Big Green.

Express comes roaring through with whistle on full
blast, their hair stands on end, seeing big wheel go
round, pushrods up and down as they pass.

Souvenirs then left behind from pennies placed on
the line and twisted copper and bronze wire made
into butterfly brooch so the girls can have some.

But definitely not for mum!

# Cooktown Times

Endeavour River Captain Cook found to rebuild
his ship after on the reef it ran aground

For some seventy days they lived in their tent town, first
Europeans establishment on this land did they found.

While Cook kept busy working on the ship from day to day
and looking through telescope for a safe passage to sail away

Banks and Parkinson made every day pay, many new
plants and the wildlife Oh so strange and new, like that
bounding Kangaroo did they sketch and record. Coloured
birds of all kinds even laughing to their mind.

To Cook, Banks must have said with pride "That
laughing bird I shall name, as "Banksaburra" "sounds
Fine." "Not so fast it's my turn today" "Kookaburra"
"will be best." Cook had needed a laugh.

Some hundred years then did pass till Mulligan in the
Palmer River gold did he discover and report, starting gold
rush by diggers of all sorts in need of a suitable seaport.

Cooktown then becomes a Boom Town. Second
biggest in Queensland to be found. Important
port of call for ships from the world around where
merchants, pubs, parlours and missions are found

The trek to Palmer is one of fate, especially when going through Hell's Gate. A rail is needed to go the easy way. A bridge across the Laura River reaches halfway. Then as they celebrate it is discovered that it's too late. Gold has petered out for Cooktown it means a turnabout

Population in decline, wartimes have their effect. Troop and Air Force move in. Convent secret code bricking headquarters to be in the know in the war to beat Tojo

Road south start of National Highway One unsealed and rough as guts, bridges there are none. Gateway to remote Cape York. You can drive to Australia's northern tip to win a bet, but could be stuck there in the wet

By the sixties population four fifty or so. Some think a shanty town, old pubs on a lean, Convent like a ghost house better days it has seen.

Outside travel by Hayles ferry once a week from Cairns, barefoot Wiggins bus once a week as well, Ansett Friendship on a par, over the Ranges most intrepid in a car.

They come only once a week on same day with intrepid travellers in dismay. That night there is a gig at West Coast pub to enjoy. Peggy on accordion, boys with tea chest, stick and string, bamboo pole with bottle tops pumping out the beat, patrons stamping feet,

Minibus tours of town and grassy Hill lookout, Hopevale Mission and Archer Point. A stop at Lion's Den pub for a beer with big python skins hogging behind the bar, see relics of old on display there, but don't expect in those days for the beer to be cold

Cooktown races big event once a year. Favourite
will win anyway, but best bet each way.

No need to disappear, our Queen and Princess Anne following
in Cook's wake on board Britannia did then visit make,
to open Convent as Cook Museum and say G'day. Town
all spruced up for big day. Road to airport made tar all the
way so she could fly off to Singapore and say hooray.

Before long tourism will have its way. Bush Pilots take Day
tour to Cooktown and three-day Cape York Tours. Aussie
Air joins in to give more people some fun. Quicksilver
ferry sails many day trippers in with happy cursing on
the way but can be rough punching it back home way.

Cooktown grows and gets in the swing; retirees move in to
enjoy relaxed lifestyle and escape the rush, going fishing a
must. Highway One now sealed to Cooktown all the way.

You can drive there and back in a day or fly with
Aussie Airways over Endeavour Reef on the way, then
see the Best of Cape York in just a few days.

Queen's Birthday long weekend crowds
roll in. Billy cart race down the hill,
fastest survivor will win. Cannon loaded,
will go off with a big bang, the crowd is
thick raffle winner lights the wick.

To Tourist Parks a caravan you can bring, on
4W Drive trip to Cape York drop in, James
Cook Museum to peruse, with Endeavour's
cannon on display. Croc Shop for souvenirs to
take away, on Endeavour River take a cruise.
New pubs, RSL and Bowls clubs add to the
joy. So come and give Cooktown a big ahoy.

# Star Wars Correspondent

*While in orbit day and night Cosmo always on the lookout
for a headline story to report that big acclaim would bring*

*Then one day the Earth stood still and across the Universe
there was a chill. In pursuit of a scoop did Cosmo swoop?*

*This event will be so great, and across the universe they can't wait.
While time on Earth will stay so still those on the Moon will feel ill.*

*There will be no day then night. For some it will be
all sunlight and dark as dark all others can see.*

*Headlines will travel at light speed for even aliens
to head. Space travel will be the shot. Without a
spaceship for a lot as the car heads for the stars.*

*But what is it that has coursed this blow Cosmo just had to
know. So at the Dark Side he had a glance. What a sock… the
Evil Emperor has sent their hex. The Dark Side is on advance.*

*They are coming no holds barred from faraway stars not just
Mars. This will be a fight to the end with not just Jedis there
to defend. The alarm has gone out; to arms is the shout.*

*"Cosmo, broadcasting for Universal Times."*

*"Our forces are in full swing and at this foe they
will through everything, we've got full heave but
will keep our secret weapon up our sleeve."*

*"Battle Taurus is full on. Our Starfighters are tacking on a mass
of Imperial Tie Fighters. The outcome is in the balance as they go
blow for blow, laser beams in ply zapping back and forth each way."*

*"Alas I must report battle Taurus is thwart, our forces
will fight next battle Leo with resolute resistance all the
way to stop them in their tracks any which way."*

*"To our allies the shout went out. Join us in this fight to save
our worlds from tyranny and lots of sin. If we don't win?"*

*"The battle of Leo rages on with no end in sight. Oh
what a fight! Win or Lose on a par, going to and fro
with each blow. No win will be all woe. Counter attacks
must be set loose there is no chance of a truce."*

*"The Death Star has been attacked and its defence
shield taken out. Before our forces were no matter
how hard they try have been forest to back out."*

*"Death Star now has Earth in range, with everyone frozen
stiff and shaking with fear. Is taking aim intent on blowing
Earth all away. Leaving just a cloud of dust and snow"*

*"Our secret defence on Mars then was deployed as Death Ray
is fired, sending eternity on its way." "Reflector Shield came
into play sending Death Ray back the other way. Death Star
took it at full blast. Destroying itself. What a laugh."*

*Verses of Another Kind*

*"Hurry, Hurry the war's end was neat, on
Earth life will now be sweet."*

*"Cosmo, Signing Off."*

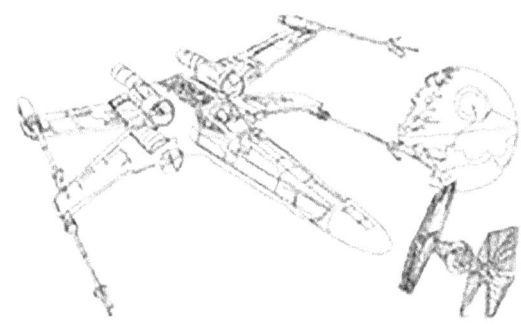

# How to Lose Friends and Alienate People

*Take them for a ride when they look to see your*
*best side, show them your thick hide*

*There could be times of need to address, best plan just be a pest*

*Then there are those who will turn up their nose,*
*just get up close treading on their toes*

*Good will is all about so give a big hooray and*
*get out of the way when asked to pay*

*For friends who you owe a favour and it's your turn to*
*lend a hand as times pass just tell'em "Kiss My Arse"*

*Those family ethics so dear to keep, do your best to be the black sheep*

*At the wedding reception when kissing the*
*bride, tell her that the groom just lied*

*In times when things get tight and community*
*works are raging get in line and keep cadging*

*When there's a line for just a few goodies so new,*
*jump the queue and say "Screw you"*

*At the party flirt around ogle passersby, be a bore more and*
*more, drink till in excess spilling vodka on ladies' dress*

*Around the pool be a hoon bomb the host and chuck a full moon*

*At the pub on mates posh in, when time to shout
back out, then on the sly be a bar fly*

*Rewards are high with two black eyes, not welcome anywhere
as times pass, instead kicked out on your fat arse*

# Rural Life

On the land can be grand

As long as one has willing hands

Then again it could be working hard

Herding sheep and in shearing shed

While making sure there are little lambs that bleat

Droving cattle way out back

Down long paddock track

Riding horseback or on tractor be

By chopper in air to muster and better see

To pen and fill up big milk tin

Cutting cane before it rains

Harvest crop of corn, rice and all

Hay bales stacked to see stock fed

Chooks must lay an egg a day

To feed us lot or get the chop

Market graders will do their best

To produce vegies and fruit, and keep out pests

On the land can be grand

But drought and flood one must withstand

# Tributes

## The Peaceful Pilot

For over twenty years my son and Heir
Has been up flying in the air
His mode of transport is mainly plains
But mother used other means
The Solomon Islands saw him pass
Searching for minerals in the grass
In New Guinea too he often flew
Making maps for me and you
Over Australia wide and bare
He surveyed high up in the air
With laser beam measuring every inch
Flying high without a flinch
Soon one of his young shoots
May follow closely in his boots
So study hard and very soon
Maybe I'll pass by on my broom

## "Flyer"

Flightless bird in the sky wings where there are none reaching high to fly the thunder heads

Do you then stretch your man-made wings to venture where eagles dare? Can I fly?

Will you lift me on your eagle's song? Will I wheel joyous in the sun's face singing songs of freedom and abandonment?

Shall I shiver in the exaltation of your flight or else remain landlocked, loveless in my dreamtime?

Wheel me high but not so lest I like I shall fall from your grace

**From my mother Beryl's book of poems**

# Happy Landing Joy

She was in love with a pilot
And he was in love with the sky
So she rang him and said come or I'll die
Ron jumped on a jet not to make her upset
And discovered their love was sublime

To Ron from Joy

In memory of Joy. My partner for seven years "Goldie"

Signed By: Ten of her lady and artist friends.

On the scarf: "I love Blue Eyes", painting of me.

# Mardi

*When only sixteen and stepmother had sway, making this young lass work and slave each day throughout. Despite her limp with a gammy leg, legacy of childhood polio bought.*

*It was time to say "hooray" from Kerang she ran away, gone missing God knows where, nowhere to be found as she quickly covered a lot of ground.*

*Across state borders hitching rides did she go, doing odd jobs to pay the way? Heading north more and more, many places did she explore?*

*Then when good highway petered out and became just dirt she had some doubt, because those bumps did hurt.*

*Now as far north as any road goes, there was no turning back, Time to by sea travel on to old TI easy as pie.*

*Being bright and alert she soon on the island welcomed and fitted in. Then it wasn't long before admirers came along and Allen did she meet turning up the heat and for life did take a wife.*

*Over coming years a family did they raise, seven children in all as things go, in building Allen made a good show while Mardi was on the go letting all know how well she could sew.*

*To her shop they all came in to have dress or shirts made or just wag the chin. Then as agent for my air charter flight she sold them left and right. Air tours to New Guinea selling strong, on occasion Mardi came along.*

*Then as things do it all went bad with Allen on the bottle and Mardi peeved off. So off she flew with Steve. To set up home in Cairns town. Woe the kids a stuck on TI, leave them there no way. So by charter flight she snatched them away.*

*For many years did they have happy days. Steve as a plasterer working for me as a builder of new homes. Mardi out to have some fun while ever the sun did shine and so our families did entwine.*

*One morning as she stretched, lifting up a cup and looked across the road where a semi-trailer stud parked she read along its side. "Kerang Transport" and of her old hometown thought.*

*Curiosity then had its way as across the road she did stray. The driver on seeing her limp his way sat up in dismay. He knew just who she was at first glance and nearly shit his pants.*

*For twenty years family had never given up hope. Drivers all over on the lookout. "You're Mardi" he exclaimed! Family reunions then the go with step mum and dad both so glad.*

*As kids grow up and leave the nest a move to a Holloways Beach unit is best, where hangis on the beach can be had with all welcome and beach dressed best.*

*Then my trade store on Murray Island is in strife with manager in my back using a knife, takes off with lots of cash and leaves a floozy in his pace. Mardi then answers the call to move in and bounce her out. And so it's done without a doubt.*

*Next it came to pass the tourist lodge on Prince of Wales Island is ready to open at last. To kick it off I'll need a good hand. Mardi to the fore giving it the all. With Steve in support housekeeping, cooking, entertaining and Spot the pet pig adding to the Gig.*

*As time is, it has its way, some drop off the perch every day and others for a bit longer get to stay. Mardi is one that did hang in there, till she landed at the Pearly Gates. Heaven beware.*

# The Port Moresby Gliding Club

A group of young enthusiasts
Met at a local pub
To talk about a common love
"The Port Moresby Gliding Club"

Their membership was very low
The running costs were high,
They needed some dramatic act
To catch the public eye.

"I've got a good idea" said one
"Been planning it all day
I'll try it out tomorrow
When coming back from Lae."

The flight to Lae was wonderful
The aircraft right on track,
They had no reason to suspect
The drama coming back.

Their business done - they climbed aboard
One had a bulging bilum
The Captain chuckled to himself,
"The last ten miles will thrill 'em"

This trick will have no impact
If I fill her up with fuel
I'll take enough for Top of Climb
And glide in from Mount Yule."

They flew along as smooth as silk
With not a single jolt
But as they got to Galley Reach
Both donks ground to a halt

The Captain said "Thank Christ they've stopped
They make a dreadful din
I'll now complete this exercise
And glide this bastard in."

A glider is a lovely thing
You see them everywhere
Some metal - others wood and glue
But never a King Air

With noses flat against the glass
The victims watched in horror
And none of them had any doubt
They'd all be dead tomorra

He held her on the centre-line
He called the Tower and said
"For Christ's sake make me number one
I'm landing straight ahead"

He put it down right on the "keys"
And made sure he was clear
Then smilingly he turned and said
"I think we need a beer"

"The Aero Club looks very nice
Looks like it's just been painted"
But there was no-one to answer him
The bloody lot had fainted

Wes turned and looked him in the eye
He said "Thank Christ that's ended
It really won't surprise me
If your licence is suspended!"

"Those passengers we've got on board
Look like they're in a trance
But now you must excuse me
Cos I think I've shit my pants"

When Joe Wal heard it on the phone
His hands flew to his head
His eyes stood out like organ stops
"F*** me" was all he said

But when he heard the details
Of this history-making flight
His eyes lit up with interest
And he thought of it all night.

For Joe had always longed to fly
Although it made him dizzy
But this bloke here could show him how
On days he wasn't busy

So Joe signed up on the spot
They headed for the pub
Now Joe's the latest member
Of the Moresby Gliding Club

Sir Jules picked up his phone and heard
A voice known far and wide,
"This Grumman that arrives next month
- I wonder how they glide"

***by Dean Darcey***

Ex-Adastra, camera operator and air traffic controller in Port Moresby at the time of this hair-raising event.

www.ingramcontent.com/pod-product-compliance
Lightning Source LLC
LaVergne TN
LVHW051225070526
838200LV00057B/4616